WITHDRAWN

Museum
Kittens

WINNETKA-NORTHFIELD
PUBLIC LIBRARY DISTRICT
WINNETKA, IL 60093
847-446-7220

Also Available:

The Mummy's Curse

Museum Kittens

The Midnight Visitor

by Holly Webb

Illustrated by Sarah Lodge

tiger tales

For the real museum cats—H.W.

For Max and Bette—S.L.

tiger tales

5 River Road, Suite 128, Wilton, CT 06897
Published in the United States 2021
Originally published in Great Britain 2020
by the Little Tiger Group
Text copyright © 2020 Holly Webb
Illustrations copyright © 2020 Sarah Lodge
Author photograph © Charlotte Knee Photography
ISBN-13: 978-1-68010-485-1
ISBN-10: 1-68010-485-3
Printed in the USA
STP/4800/0422/0821
All rights reserved
10 9 8 7 6 5 4 3 2 1

www.tigertalesbooks.com

Contents

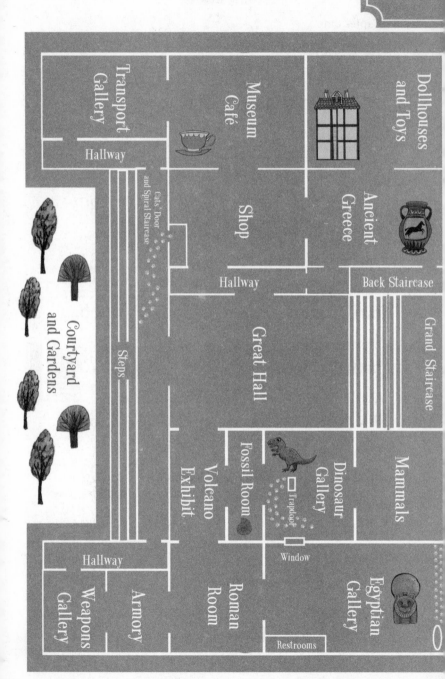

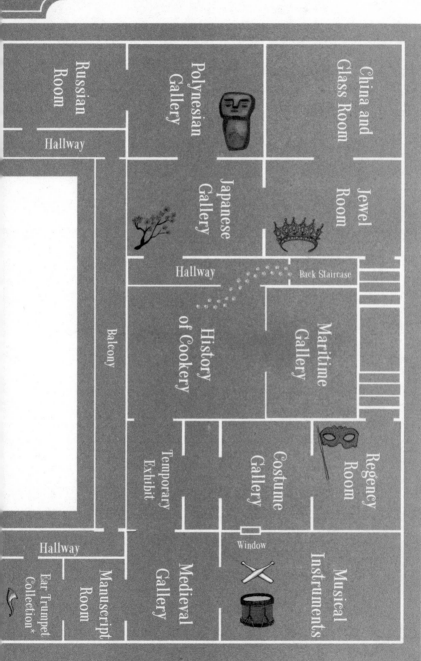

Map

First Floor

Russian Room

Hallway

Polynesian Gallery

China and Glass Room

Jewel Room

Japanese Gallery

Hallway

Back Staircase

Balcony

History of Cookery

Maritime Gallery

Temporary Exhibit

Costume Gallery

Regency Room

Window

Hallway

Ear Trumpet Collection*

Manuscript Room

Medieval Gallery

Musical Instruments

rs. Jane Martlesham Bequest

❦ Chapter One ❦

The Kittens

"Mrrrowww." Tasha rolled over and waved her tiny striped paws in the air. The wide stone steps that led up to the museum entrance were warm from the sun, and she was so sleepy. There was a light breeze blowing off the river, and she could hear gulls calling over the water.

"You're getting your fur dirty, Tasha,"

said a disapproving voice, and the tabby kitten opened one green eye to see who was talking to her. "Ma says we shouldn't get our fur dirty—we should be clean and neat at all times."

"Oh, hush, Bianca." Tasha closed her eye again, but it was no good. Her sister was still there—she could feel her. Bianca was blocking out the spring sunshine, and now the afternoon felt dull and chilly.

"Ma says," Bianca insisted. She sat down next to Tasha and started to wash herself. She didn't need to—her white fur was spotless as always. Even her paw pads were perfectly pink, and it looked as though she'd combed her beautiful whiskers.

Tasha rolled over and sprang up, peering over her shoulder at her gray and black tabby stripes. Bianca was right. She was covered in dust, and her fur was sticking up all over the place. Half of her whiskers seemed to be stuck together, too—she wasn't sure how that had happened. She had gone exploring in the museum workshop earlier in the day. Maybe she shouldn't have looked so closely at that pot of varnish. She stuck out her tongue to try to reach her sticky whiskers, but it didn't work.

"You are a disgrace to the museum," Bianca said, stopping mid wash with one paw in the air. "Just look at you. Huh."

"I'm not!" Tasha said, annoyed. "We're supposed to be here to keep the mice and rats away. The rats don't care if my whiskers are tangled. It doesn't matter if I'm clean or not."

"Ma won't agree," Bianca purred, twitching her whiskers at a pair of visitors walking past them up the steps. "See? They thought I was adorable. They just said so. They didn't even notice you."

Tasha considered leaping on her sister's head and rolling her over in the dust. Then she wouldn't be so perfect.

But Tasha would only get into trouble. Ma might keep her downstairs in the basement in the museum cats' den until bedtime, instead of letting her explore the museum and the courtyard and the gardens with the others.

"Come here," Bianca sighed, leaning over to lick the scruffy fur on Tasha's back. "I'll clean you up."

Tasha's whiskers bristled as Bianca licked her fur straight. She sat hunched over with her ears flat back, letting out little outraged hisses.

"Don't make such a fuss! If you don't like being washed, you shouldn't get yourself in such a mess."

That did it! Tasha was going to have to jump on her now, even if it meant staying in the basement for weeks.

Just as she was about to pounce, their brother Boris hopped down the steps and bumped noses with Tasha. "Don't even *think* about doing that to me," he told Bianca with a yawn. "It's bad enough when Ma makes me wash my ears."

Bianca looked his orange tabby coat up and down and sniffed. "You're almost clean, I suppose." Then she sighed again at Tasha. All the pieces of fur she'd licked clean and straight were starting to stick out already. "I give up," she muttered.

"Good! Oh, look, more visitors."

All three kittens tried to look charming—sometimes the visitors had snacks to share. But as usual, the visitors only made a big deal over Bianca. Tasha watched, wondering how her sister did it, and Boris settled down for a nap halfway off a step.

"White kittens are very unusual," Bianca purred as the visitors walked on up to the museum entrance. "You two are … common."

"Hey!" Boris opened one eye. "Orange tabby stripes are handsome. Ma said so. I wouldn't want to be a white cat."

Bianca's blue eyes glittered. "And why not?" she hissed.

"Camouflage." Boris nodded knowingly. "I mean, you don't have any. You stick out. Tasha and I can slink into the shadows and hide because we have stripes."

"Well, I don't want to slink." Bianca sat up straighter and set her ears at the perkiest angle possible. "I am beautiful, and I want everyone to see me." Then she frowned, her muzzle wrinkling as she looked at the dark dots spattering the terrace. "Ugh! It's *raining*! I'll get wet!" A large raindrop splashed down next to Bianca's delicate paws, and her tail fluffed up in horror. The white kitten dashed up the steps and bolted across the terrace to the neat little door hidden behind one of the columns.

The museum building was very grand, with stone columns all along the front and statues on either side of all the doors. Even the cats' door had its own little statue—a marble cat perched on the doorframe peering down. Its nose was almost rubbed away by hundreds of silky tails brushing past over the years.

As Bianca disappeared underneath the statue, a fluffy gray cat with a full fan of white whiskers appeared in the doorway and stepped out onto the terrace. Tasha thought about pretending not to have noticed her mother and darting off across the courtyard, but it wouldn't work. Smokey was a famous hunter, and her green eyes were sharp. She'd know right away that Tasha had seen her.

"There's Ma looking for us," Boris groaned, and he and Tasha hopped up the steps and padded over to the gray cat.

"Can we please stay out a little longer?" Tasha pleaded. "It can't be even close to bedtime."

Smokey narrowed her eyes, peering up at the sky, and nudged noses with Tasha. "It's getting late, kitten. And it's wet. Come on inside. It's almost time for dinner. The Night Guard brought us fish today as a treat."

The Night Guard was one of the museum's guards, and he was in charge of feeding the cats. He was grumpy and sometimes shouted at the kittens when they got in his way, but Ma said that was only because his legs hurt.

Boris's whiskers fanned out, trembling with excitement. "Fish! Come on, Tasha! We need to get down there first, before everyone nabs it."

The two kittens barged through the little door—they weren't quite tall enough for their tails to rub the stone cat's nose yet—and padded down the stairs to their shadowy home.

❧ Chapter Two ❧

The New Arrival

The museum's basement storerooms went
on a very long way underground. Even
the kittens' grandfather, the fearsome
white cat Ivan, hadn't explored them all.
They were full of boxes and chests and
trunks of ancient museum treasures that
almost everyone had forgotten about.

The cats lived in the basement at
the front of the building, with a spiral

staircase leading up to the small door on the terrace. There was a sloping tunnel that led up into the Egyptian Gallery, too, and opened out behind a large and musty-smelling mummy case, as well as many other hallways and chutes and hiding spots that the cats used to get around.

Tasha, Bianca, and Boris were asleep on an old tapestry full of holes, their tummies full of fish, with Smokey curled lovingly around them.

It was the dark of night, and the
shower that had spattered down
on the terrace that afternoon
had turned into a storm. The
wind rattled through the old
chimneys and air ducts with shrill
little whines and angry growls,
and rain was lashing against the
walls. Even safe underground,
the kittens stirred and shifted
uneasily in their sleep.

Tasha woke with a squeal as
something banged loudly on the door
at the top of the spiral staircase. The
noise seemed to echo around the
basement, and her fur prickled with
fear. What was happening? That
door should be shut tight.

There were cats out on duty in the museum, of course, prowling around the priceless objects in the galleries upstairs. They were on watch for mice and rats, or even burglars. But the cat guards knew to slide silently in and out of their den. This was an intruder!

"Stay here!" Smokey hissed, her green eyes glinting fiercely at her children in the soft light from the doorway. "I'll be back soon." Then she shot away, joining the tide of tabby and white and orange fur surging out of the sleeping quarters toward that strange, suspicious noise.

The kittens stayed huddled together on the tapestry, feeling the warmth of their mother's body fade away.

Tasha's tail was swishing anxiously

from side to side. "I want to see what's happening…."

"Ma said to stay," Bianca mewed.

"We could just look around the door," suggested Boris, standing up. "That wouldn't do any harm, would it?"

Tasha jumped up with an eager nod.

Bianca shuffled her paws worriedly, and then sprang down from the tapestry after Tasha and Boris. She didn't want to be left behind. All three kittens peered around the doorframe, trying to see farther up the hallway. In the dim light of the lamps, they could just make out the spiral staircase, with shadowy cats standing at attention all the way up the steps. They were as still as statues, but Tasha could hear the soft hiss of their breathing.

They couldn't see the door at the top.

"I want to know what it was!" Tasha's tail was flicking back and forth now, and her ears were flattened. "It's important, I know it is."

"No...," Bianca moaned, but the other two were already creeping along the hallway.

Tasha started to weave her way up the staircase, between the cats. There were a few hisses of annoyance as her brother and sister followed, but no one stopped the three kittens as they padded toward their mother and grandfather, who were standing together one step from the top.

"I thought you told them to stay in the den," Grandpa Ivan muttered to Smokey, his one eye narrowing, and she sighed.

"I did. I should have known you naughty kittens wouldn't listen. Now stay by me, you three, and don't move!" Then Smokey turned back to watching the heavy wooden door at the top of the stairs. The two cats on guard duty were pulling back the heavy bolts with their teeth.

Tasha shivered and pressed tight against her mother as the door opened a crack and the wind battered and shrieked against the dark timbers. All the cats on the stairs hissed, lowering their heads into the wind, feeling it lick their fur on end and tie their tails in knots.

The door swung fully open, and a haze of damp air rushed in. Outside, the cats could see the rain lashing the flagstones on the terrace, each heavy drop striking up a little fountain as it landed. It was midnight-black out there, and even the cats' night eyes were blind. The two cat guards took a cautious step forward, and one of them bellowed, "Who goes there?"

"Identify yourself!" the other guard roared, not to be outdone.

There was a faint thickening of the darkness outside the door, and then another cat appeared, a skinny, elderly cat who looked even skinnier with the rain flattening his coat over his bones. His dark tabby stripes seemed to melt into the shadows around the doorway. Something about him made the two guards fall back, pressing themselves respectfully against the doorframe to let him pass.

The cats on the stairs peered forward, staring at the elderly tabby and waiting for him to speak.

But he didn't. He couldn't, Tasha and the others realized, because there was something in his mouth. A little saggy something, all black and bedraggled.

The elderly cat padded carefully down the top step and stood in front of Smokey and her kittens. Then he leaned down and laid the soggy ball of fur at her feet. He nodded slowly and then turned around, stepped onto the landing, and disappeared out into the rain-soaked night, still silent.

On the stairs, the wet ball of dark fur wriggled and sneezed and sat up, staring at Smokey and the kittens with emerald eyes.

"I'm Peter," squeaked the small black kitten, gazing nervously around at the rows and rows of cats. "Hello."

🐾 Chapter Three 🐾

The First Night

"*Who was that?*" The whisper ran around the stairs, and the two guard cats hurried out onto the terrace to call the elderly tabby back. But they returned looking downcast.

"No sign of him."

The little black kitten laid his ears flat and shuffled his paws. "He—um—he said he was taking me to my new home…."

A disapproving chorus echoed around the stairs at once.

"Here?"

"The little tadpole wants to stay!"

"Well, I'm not sure about that!"

"Quiet!" Grandpa Ivan let out a loud, growly meow. "The museum is a home for all cats in need—you know that quite well. Besides, I've seen that elderly tabby fellow before. Around and about. He's a sensible creature. If he brought the kitten here, then here he stays."

Smokey came up beside Ivan and gently licked the black kitten's ears. "You must be so tired," she said to him gently. "Come back down to the basement with us and sleep. The warmth from the hot-water pipes will dry your fur. You can tell us where you came from in the morning."

The rows of cats parted like a wave rolling back as she nudged the little black kitten down the stairs toward the basement. She half lifted him onto the pile of old tapestries where Tasha and Bianca and Boris slept with her every night, and the three kittens followed. They lay down next to him, but it felt so odd curling up with their mother and a stranger.

Tasha lay there, her eyes half open, peering at the newcomer. She felt sorry for him, of course, being so cold and wet and lonely. But he didn't smell like a museum kitten.

When they woke up the next morning,
the three kittens were snuggled up in
Smokey's long gray fur, just like always.
The black kitten was curled in a tiny ball
at the very edge of the tapestries,
all alone.

After breakfast and washing, Smokey
tried to coax him to tell his story. Tasha
sat beside her mother, watching eagerly.
The most interesting part of living in a
museum was all the stories that came
with the treasures in the galleries, but a
story she hadn't heard before was the very
best kind. She was sure that the black
kitten's adventures would be exciting.
After all, he'd come from Out There.

But when the black kitten had licked
breakfast off his whiskers at last and

settled down to be questioned, he didn't seem to have a story to tell at all. He didn't know anything, except that his name was Peter, and that Herring, the elderly tabby, hadn't been his father or his grandfather. Just someone who had taken care of him for as long he could remember and had brought him to the museum.

He sat in the middle of a circle of curious cats, his whiskers drooping as he failed to answer question after question.

"What was your mother's name?"

"Were you born here in the city?"

"Do you have any brothers or sisters?"

In the end, they gave up. There was no chance of sending Peter away, of course. He would be a museum cat, like all the others. But he was a strange one. He didn't seem to fit in, and the black kitten knew it.

"Leave the poor creature alone,"
Grandpa Ivan ordered. "If he doesn't
know, then he doesn't know. Maybe he'll
remember in time." He fixed Tasha, Boris,
and Bianca with a stern glare. "You young
ones must show him around." Tasha was
never sure how her grandfather could
look so much more fiercely with one eye
than everyone else did with two, but he
managed it. "Make him feel at home.
Show him the ropes!"

"What ropes?" Boris muttered in
Tasha's ear. "Does he mean the sailors'
knot collection in the Maritime Gallery?
Why do we have to show this scrawny kit
those?"

"Shh!" Tasha hissed back. Even though
both of Grandpa Ivan's ears looked

chewed and he was deaf in one ear, she was almost sure he'd heard Boris being rude. His whiskers were bristling.

Maybe Peter would like to see around the museum, she thought hopefully. Maybe he'd like the same rooms she did. They could show him the fossilized fish, and the lion statues, and the shudderingly scary cat mummies in the Egyptian Gallery.

"Come on," Bianca said a little haughtily—but not too haughtily, because she was scared of Grandpa Ivan, too. No one knew exactly how he'd lost his eye and all those pieces of his ears…. "This way!"

🐾 Chapter Four 🐾

Exploring

Peter obediently followed the three kittens through the galleries. Herring had told him that the museum was a strange place, full of treasures. "Though a lot of it's just old junk," the elderly tabby cat had added, chuckling. "Dusty old bones, not a scrap of meat on them."

Peter wasn't sure about the bones, either, but the visitors certainly seemed

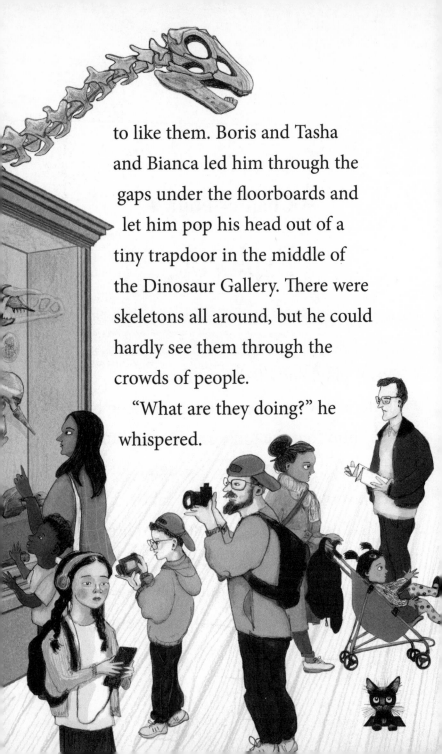

to like them. Boris and Tasha
and Bianca led him through the
gaps under the floorboards and
let him pop his head out of a
tiny trapdoor in the middle of
the Dinosaur Gallery. There were
skeletons all around, but he could
hardly see them through the
crowds of people.

"What are they doing?" he
whispered.

The three kittens stared at him. "Visiting," Tasha said at last. "It's what they do. They look at things."

"They take a lot of pictures," Bianca added. "Most of them take pictures of me," she added smugly.

Tasha rolled her eyes and saw Peter glance at her. "She's very spoiled," she whispered to him. "She loves having her picture taken."

"Come on!" Boris was already heading back down the tunnel. "I want to show him the swords."

"No," Bianca hissed. "The jewelry is much more interesting. There are six crowns," she added impressively to Peter, who nodded, wide-eyed.

"Boring sparkly stuff," Boris grunted, but he followed the others, slipping along the corridors and around the display cases to the Jewel Room.

"Keep hidden!" Bianca snapped. She batted Peter back into the shadows with one small white paw as he stopped to gaze up at the enormous marble staircase in the

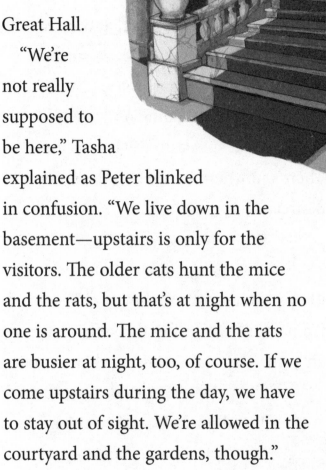

Great Hall.

"We're not really supposed to be here," Tasha explained as Peter blinked in confusion. "We live down in the basement—upstairs is only for the visitors. The older cats hunt the mice and the rats, but that's at night when no one is around. The mice and the rats are busier at night, too, of course. If we come upstairs during the day, we have to stay out of sight. We're allowed in the courtyard and the gardens, though."

"I'm good at hiding," Peter said eagerly, and Boris snorted.

"Not as if there's much of you to hide,"

43

he said, looking Peter over, and Peter scrunched himself down even smaller.

Tasha glared at her brother, but he didn't notice. "Come on," she told Peter. "We'll sneak up the back stairs. There's nowhere to hide on the Grand Staircase."

They peered down at the Jewel Room from above, squinting through a latticed air vent. The crowns and necklaces and diamond-encrusted eggs were all locked away in thick glass cases, but they still flashed and glittered in the sunlight from the tall windows.

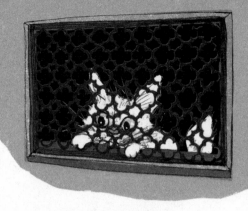

They left
Bianca there
in the end, her
little pink nose
poking through the vent to get as close
to the jewels as she could. One of these
days, she would have a diamond tiara of
her own, or maybe a pearl necklace.

"Now let's see the weapons," Boris
commanded, marching along a drafty
hallway that led around the courtyard
to the next building. "Best room in the
whole place."

"Oh, it isn't!" Tasha stopped, staring at
him.

"What's your favorite?" Peter asked her,
and the tabby kitten's whiskers shook as
she tried to think.

"I'm not sure…," she admitted at last. "I love them all."

"Typical," muttered Boris, looking back at them both.

"I mean … the Egyptian Gallery … and the dollhouses … and then there's the mosaics…. I just can't choose."

"That's because you spend all your time daydreaming about who those tattered old things belonged to." Boris gave a big sigh. "Let's go. There! Look! Isn't that impressive?"

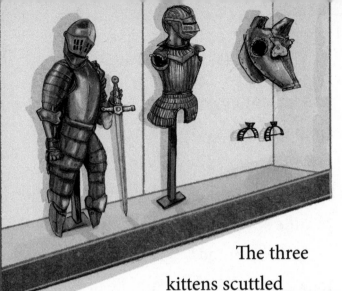

The three
kittens scuttled
behind an open door and
peered around at the suits of armor
standing guard around the room. They
were eerie, Peter thought, waiting there
with their metal gauntlets on their
swords. He wouldn't like to peer under
the visors on those helmets, in case he
found something else looking back at
him.

"They're amazing," he agreed,
hoping to make Boris happy. But that

only meant he got a long tour, sneaking
from case to case to inspect all of Boris's
favorite swords. Boris was particularly
fond of the Japanese ones, and Peter had
to stifle several yawns.

"Are you bored?" Tasha whispered
in his ear, right in the middle of Boris's
lecture on Samurai armor.

Peter twitched. He was, but he didn't
like to say so. What if Tasha didn't like
him saying that her brother was boring?

"Boris, can you smell that?" Tasha
sniffed thoughtfully. "What is it, do you
think? Egg salad, maybe? Or tuna?"

"Sandwiches?" Boris abandoned the
Samurai and gazed around the gallery, his
whiskers stretched out like great white
fans. "Just a minute." He crouched low

and padded away, ears turning slowly as he tracked imaginary sandwiches.

"I couldn't smell anything," Peter said, frowning. He was proud of his sense of smell—he could sniff out a tasty piece of bacon several garbage cans away.

"Oh, neither could I. But you can always distract Boris with sandwiches. They're his favorite thing. Especially if he's sneaked them—he says they taste better if they're stolen. He's always raiding the garbage cans in the museum café."

Peter wrinkled his muzzle. The canned food that the Night Guard had put down for them at breakfast had been so good, and there had been so much of it, even with all those cats to feed. He'd always had not-quite-enough food when he and Herring had been wandering around the city. He wondered if Boris had ever been hungry. The orange kitten certainly made sure he got more than his fair share at meal times—Peter didn't think he'd ever seen anyone eat faster.

"Look out!" Tasha hissed suddenly, interrupting his thoughts. "Visitors! We're not supposed to be in here. Run!"

She skittered away into the shadows, behind the huge armored elephant. Peter looked around wildly. He could hear footsteps and voices getting closer and closer. It sounded like a great stampeding crowd. What if he was seen in the galleries? Would he be thrown out of the museum, after all Herring had done to get him here?

Peter stood frozen at the feet of the
Samurai warrior, his tail fluffing to
three times its size. Then, as
the voices grew louder,
he gave a tiny mew
of panic and shot
upward, inside
the plated leather
armor. If there
was a ghostly
warrior inside,
it was going to
get an awful
shock….

He clung on tight to the ribbed metal, his heart thumping as the visitors talked and talked only a whisker or so away. What if they loved the Samurai soldiers as much as Boris did? He could be here for hours!

The sharp metal plates felt as if they were going to cut his claws in half. Were the visitors still there? The voices seemed to have moved farther away—and now he could hardly hear them. Slowly, slowly, Peter crept back down and peeked out beneath the heavy armor-plated skirts.

The visitors were gone, but so were the other kittens.

"Tasha?" he called hopefully, glancing around the gallery. "Are you there? Boris?"

A faint echo whispered through the suits of armor, but that was all. Peter shuddered as the dark emptiness behind the visors seemed to turn toward him and scooted for the door.

He wasn't going to stay here to be eaten by long-dead warriors, he decided. If Tasha and Boris had abandoned him, he would just have to explore by himself.

❦ Chapter Five ❦

Trouble Fitting In

All through that first day, the older cats whispered as they curled up together, or set out on their guard duties. Even though Grandpa Ivan had said Peter must be allowed to stay, there was still a great deal of gossiping to be done. Whenever Peter padded past, exploring his new home, hissy little whispers followed him. The cats put their heads together and muttered.

No one knew how old the strange black kitten was, for starters. He was quite a bit smaller than Boris, but then Boris was huge; everyone said so. He was almost as tall as Bianca and Tasha but he was thinner, as though he'd never been properly fed. He kept appearing here and there, always hunched over or half hidden behind a box or a pile of papers. He was quiet, too, now that he knew he had to be. He could slip through the hallways and galleries like a shadow.

"He's too quiet," Bianca said later that afternoon as the shadows were gathering along the terrace outside the Egyptian Gallery. "I don't like it. He's such a sly little thing. I'll bet he's off somewhere sniffing around where he isn't wanted."

"Or he's checking out the museum's treasures," Boris suggested. "What do we really know about that elderly tabby cat who brought him here? He could be a master criminal, and Peter is his cat on the inside."

Tasha was still feeling guilty about abandoning Peter earlier. She should have gone back to the Weapons Gallery to find him. Should she look for him now and say she's sorry? Or would that just make it worse? She was only half listening to Bianca and Boris, so she didn't argue with them for once. Afterward she wished she had, because as soon as Bianca had wandered off to flutter her whiskers at a visitor and Boris had gone to ask when dinner would be, a small dark shape stole

out from behind
a statue of a lion
goddess and slunk
away. Tasha sat
watching from the
terrace with her
mouth open, but all her
words were frozen.

*It's just Bianca and Boris—you don't
need to worry about them. I never do,*
she should have said. Or, *I wish I hadn't
left you behind in the Weapons Gallery. I
didn't mean to. I was just scared that we'd
get into trouble....*

She tried to be friendly—that night,
she left a space on their pile of tapestries
for the black kitten to sleep. But instead,
he huddled himself up inside an old

57

wooden jewelry box, all on his own. Tasha lay there in the dark, watching him and worrying.

The black kitten didn't notice that Tasha was peering at him over Boris's large orange tail. He was squished into the tiny jewelry box, the worn velvet lining soft under his paws. He was very comfortable, and he wasn't hungry. He was warm and dry, and Grandpa Ivan had said he could stay.

But he didn't belong. Not like the others. Clever, funny Tasha, and Bianca who melted all the visitors' hearts. And Boris, who was obviously going to be the biggest, fiercest, most rat-scaring cat in the history of the museum.

Peter sniffed, and sighed, and turned around in the tiny box—which was extremely difficult. *Maybe things will be better tomorrow,* he thought hopefully as his head nodded lower onto the edge of the box. *Maybe tomorrow, things will be different....*

"Are you sure you're even a cat?" Boris peered down, his whiskers brushing the little black kitten's nose. He was looking sideways at Bianca and Tasha, wanting them to laugh along.

"What?" Peter blinked. "Of course I'm a cat."

"Are you? Really? I mean, you don't know anything else about yourself. Maybe you're a skinny little ferret." Boris snickered, thinking that he was being very clever and funny. "Or maybe you're a rat. I've seen rats bigger than you!"

Peter shuddered. He had seen rats, too, while he was out on the streets with Herring. Their yellow teeth and glittering eyes would be stuck in his memory forever.

"Leave him alone," Tasha growled. "You aren't funny, Boris.

Maybe you're an elephant! Stop being mean."

Peter was still thinking about rats and hardly heard her. But he heard Bianca laughing, a high, squeaky little laugh that made him feel hot and embarrassed and miserable all over. His ears flattened and his tail drooped, and he skulked silently away from the three kittens.

"Go on, rat cat!" Boris called after him, snorting with laughter, and Peter hung his head. He'd really thought that today might be better. Today was supposed to be the day that he found a way to fit in. How could he ever be a real museum cat when he knew nothing about who he was, or where he came from? All the others had been born at the museum—they were never going to let him be one of them. Wherever he went in the galleries, there seemed to be a true museum cat peering down its nose at him.

He couldn't stay.

Peter slunk through the Dinosaur Gallery like a tiny patch of shadow and crept into a room full of stuffed animals. None of the museum cats liked this room much—it smelled strange, and there were too many large creatures with teeth. The enormous she-wolf by the door made him feel nervous. But in here, he had a good chance of being left alone to figure out what he was going to do. He settled down behind a glass case with a saber-toothed tiger in it and began to wash slowly. It helped him think.

Herring had told Peter that the
museum was a safe place, where cats
were well cared for, and Peter could see
that this was true. He had been very well
fed. He closed his eyes for a moment,

blissfully remembering the treat of cold chicken that the Night Guard had put down as part of their dinner the night before. It made his whiskers quivery just thinking about it. And he was warm and dry, with a comfortable place to sleep. Even though he had woken up feeling as if the jewelry box had given him corners!

But it wasn't enough. Smokey licked his ears affectionately whenever she strolled past, but no one talked to him. No one curled up around him to keep him safe in the dark, the way Herring had. And before that, someone had loved him. Peter couldn't remember his mother or father, or his brothers and sisters, but he knew he must have had a family, once.

He almost remembered someone licking him gently as he fell asleep.

The museum was a place to stay, but that didn't make it a home. Peter stopped licking his paws and breathed out a tiny sigh. He didn't want to leave the good food and the warm bed and go back to wandering the streets. Especially not on his own.

But wasn't a home worth hunting for?

Chapter Six

Secrets

Peter was still sitting behind the saber-toothed tiger, trying to come up with a plan, when a scuffling noise made him jump. He peered out from behind the glass case, hoping that it wasn't one of the enormous rats that Boris had enjoyed telling him about on their tour.

It wasn't a rat. Staring back at him with wide panicked eyes was Tasha, her fur all on end and her whiskers bristling.

"What's the matter?" he gasped. "Are you all right?" The tabby kitten looked terrified, as though something was after her. Peter glanced worriedly around the gallery, wondering what it could be.

"Oh…. It's you." Tasha panted. The fur along her spine flattened down a little, and she took a deep breath. "I thought…. Oh, dear." She padded her front paws up and down, looking embarrassed.

"Is someone chasing you?" Peter asked, his whiskers flicking anxiously back and forth.

Tasha shook her head slowly. "No…." She looked behind her and then edged a little closer to the tiger case. "Promise you won't tell the others?"

Peter felt something inside him swell up like a little balloon. A secret! Between him and Tasha!

"I promise," he said earnestly, hoping and hoping it wasn't some horrible trick that Boris or Bianca had put her up to.

"I'm-really-scared-of-the-wolf," Tasha jabbered.

"Oh…." Peter looked over at the entrance to the gallery, where the huge stuffed wolf stood on a high wooden block, baring her teeth. He could almost hear her growling from here, even though he knew she was stuffed. "Me, too."

"Really?" Tasha said, sounding surprised and a little bit relieved. "I didn't think you would be. I mean, you've been a street cat—you've seen tons of scary things, I bet."

Peter nodded. "That's why I'm scared of the wolf—it looks exactly like the enormous German shepherd that chased me and Herring for miles and miles one night. We only got away because we scrambled up a fire escape and hid behind some chimneys. The dog couldn't follow us up onto the roof, but we had to stay there until morning."

"Ugh." Tasha shuddered and closed her eyes. "I don't even want to think about it."

"I'm sorry. I didn't mean to make it worse," Peter told her apologetically. Then he wrinkled his nose. "But why did you come in here if you don't like the wolf?"

"To find you, of course." Tasha leaned forward and dabbed noses with him. Peter was so surprised that he almost darted back behind the saber-toothed tiger.

"To find me?" he squeaked.

"Yes. I wanted to say I shouldn't have run off and left you in the Weapons Gallery yesterday. I'm so sorry. And I'm sorry that Boris is so horrible. He's my brother, and I'm absolutely ashamed of him. And Bianca isn't much better."

"Oh…." Peter stared at her. He hadn't expected that at all.

"I think Boris might actually be a little jealous," Tasha went on. "He's never lived outside the museum, or had any grand adventures. All he does is skulk around, trying to steal snacks."

"Um—I haven't had any grand adventures, either," Peter pointed out humbly.

"Yes, you have!" Tasha was practically bouncing up and down on her paws.

"You arrived at the museum in the middle of a dark and stormy night! And no one knows where you came from!"

"Even I don't know," Peter said, gazing glumly at the floor. "It's horrible. Like I don't belong anywhere."

"Really? Is that how you feel?" Tasha's green eyes widened. "I thought it was exciting and wonderful and mysterious."

Peter sat up a little straighter and felt his whiskers curl a little. "Mysterious?"

"Oh, yes. I'm extremely jealous, and I think Boris is, too." Then she looked at him anxiously. "I knew Boris and Bianca

were being horrible, but I never realized
that they were making you feel like you
didn't belong here. I know everyone
keeps whispering about you, but it's not
only because you're new—and different!
It's not up to them! Grandpa Ivan said the
museum was for *every* cat. You … you
are going to stay, aren't you? Do you like
it enough to stay?" She ducked her head
shyly. "Do you like *us*?"

"I *was* thinking about leaving," Peter
admitted. "I was trying to make a plan.
But I don't know the city very well. When
we were traveling here, I just followed
Herring. So I wasn't sure how to go about
finding my real home."

"*This* is your real home," Tasha said
firmly. "You *do* belong."

Peter shuffled his paws sadly. "But I'm so little and skinny," he muttered. "And there aren't any other black cats at the museum. No one is like me. And—" he looked around secretively and then whispered—"I've never caught a rat. Not even a mouse, actually."

"Oh, well, neither have I," Tasha admitted. "Ma says we're not old enough. There are rats in some of the galleries that are bigger than Boris."

Peter stared at her, not sure whether to be relieved or not.

"So Boris hasn't caught one, either?" he asked.

"Nope. We have a toy one that a little girl gave to Bianca. But it has a tail made of feathers." Tasha rolled her eyes. "The visitors are very strange sometimes. Imagine not knowing the difference between a mouse and a bird!"

"I thought you all must have done a lot of guard work at the museum," Peter muttered, his eyes brightening.

"We're just starting to learn," Tasha told him. "Sometimes Ma gives us lessons, and so does Grandpa Ivan, but he says we're absolutely useless. If you did catch a rat, would it make you feel better?"

Peter swallowed hard, thinking of glittering eyes, sharp yellow teeth, and whip-like tails, but he nodded. "Yes."

Tasha nodded determinedly. "All right. Then that's what we'll do."

🐾 Chapter Seven 🐾

Making Friends

They'd been creeping stealthily in and out of the galleries for hours, searching for even a sniff of a rat, and Peter's paws were starting to ache. Luckily, the Egyptian Gallery seemed to be clear of visitors just now. It was lunchtime, Tasha had explained, when most of the visitors decided they needed to stop by the café for a little something to keep them going.

"Are you sure there are rats in the museum?" Peter asked, sitting down next to a huge pink granite lion for a rest.

"Oh, yes." Tasha nodded firmly—and then she looked around all the statues and sighed. "They're always causing trouble. We see them in hallways every so often, but they always scuttle off. They try and sneak in the kitchens of the museum café and eat the cupcakes, but the worst thing is, they eat the treasures sometimes, too."

She leaned close to Peter and whispered darkly, "There's a beautiful silk kimono in the Japanese Gallery with cherry blossoms and cherries embroidered all over it. Except if you look closely, it's covered in little holes where the rats nibbled the cherries right off!"

"But silk cherries don't taste like anything, do they?" Peter frowned.

"Of course not. But rats are too clueless to figure that out."

The two kittens didn't see the flicker of a long, pink tail over in the corner behind a stone pharaoh. They didn't hear a sharp hiss of indrawn breath or the scurrying of paws as a very insulted rat hurried away to tell all of his friends what he'd just heard.

Peter shook his head. "I don't think there are any rats left. Maybe your mother and grandfather and aunts and uncles are just such good rat-catchers that all of the rats are gone! We haven't seen a single one. Not even a mouse, either."

"Maybe." Tasha sighed. "We have been looking for a while." She glanced behind her to check that no visitors were around, and then she hopped up onto the lion's concrete base and settled in between his hind paws, where there was a comfy little nook. She slumped over the stone and looked down at Peter.

Peter watched her anxiously. They'd been chasing each other around the museum all afternoon, and the tabby kitten looked grumpy. Was she wishing that she hadn't offered to help? Had she changed her mind, and now she wanted him to go away?

Sadly, he started to shuffle backward away from Tasha and the pink stone lion, but then she leaned over the lion's paw and asked, "Where are you going? Why don't you come up here? This lion is nice to sit on, but he's chilly."

"Oh!" Peter's ears twitched back up, and he jumped onto the statue next to her.

"This is an Egyptian king, you know," Tasha told him chattily as he snuggled down next to her. "They liked cats. This one pretended he was a lion. Two lions, actually. There's another one of him over there."

"That's … odd." Peter looked up at the lion's face. The statue was certainly amazing. But he wasn't sure how a king could think he was two huge cats at once.

"You'll get used to it. The museum is full of odd things. There's a statue over there with a human body and a cat's head. No tail, though, which is a little silly. I'd really miss my tail."

"Me, too." Peter flicked his tail so that it lay next to the lion's huge stone one. "Thank you for looking for rats with me."

"I just wish we'd found one." Tasha shook her whiskers. "Where are they all? That's what I want to know."

"You two had better not fall asleep up there!"

Peter and Tasha popped their heads over the lion's paws and peered down at Grandpa Ivan. The elderly white cat was sitting in front of the statue, gazing up at them from under his huge, furry eyebrows.

"There's a big party of visitors that's just about to walk by, and you look like you're settling in for a nap. Come on down."

"Oops. We're sorry, Grandpa." Tasha hopped off the pink lion to land next to him, and Peter leaped after her.

"You can come and sit with me instead," Grandpa Ivan suggested. "I haven't had a chance to talk to you yet, youngster."

Tasha's eyes widened, and Peter

glanced at her worriedly. Grandpa
Ivan wanted to talk to him? He was
the oldest cat in the museum, and
a fearsome warrior. Boris had
already boasted to Peter about
his grandfather's amazing rat-
catching exploits. What would
such a famous cat want to talk
to a skinny little kitten for?

"Make sure you shout in his
left ear," Tasha hissed at him
as they followed Grandpa Ivan
through a neat little doorway in
the corner of the Egyptian Gallery
behind the mummy case and
trotted down the hallway to the
basement. "He's deaf."

"I heard that, miss!" the elderly cat snapped back. "Not so deaf that you can get anything past me."

Tasha looked shocked, and the two kittens went the rest of the way to the basement den in silence.

"So, you're befriending our new arrival?" Grandpa Ivan asked once he'd padded himself a warm little nest in a pile of velvet curtains. He looked down at the two kittens sitting politely in front of him, his blue-green eye narrowing. "Making sure he knows his way around?"

"Yes, Grandpa."

"Good, good…. And you, whatsyername…."

"Peter," Tasha put in helpfully, and her

grandfather glowered at her.

"I knew that! Whatsyername, like I said, how are you finding the museum?"

"It's very beautiful," Peter said nervously.

"My grandkittens taking care of you?"

"Um…." Peter gave Tasha an anxious look. What should he say? Grandpa Ivan looked as though he could smell a lie at fifty tail-lengths, but he couldn't say that Boris and Bianca were being mean, could he?

"Hmmm. That orange grandson of mine giving you a hard time, is he? Don't you listen to him, whatsyername. He'll be a loyal friend once you've won him over, I promise you that. And as for Little Miss Bianca, she's not as feather-witted as she seems to be."

"Grandpa," Tasha put in. "What's happened to all the rats?"

"What?" Grandpa Ivan peered down at her. "What are you talking about, tabby-one-whose-name'll-come-to-me-in-a-minute?"

"We can't find any. We've looked everywhere. Do you think they left? Maybe there aren't any rats in the museum anymore."

The two kittens stared at Grandpa Ivan and he stared back, wide-eyed. Then he started to make a strange wheezing, coughing noise. Tasha and Peter exchanged worried looks, and then they realized. Grandpa Ivan was laughing.

"I don't think it's funny," Peter
whispered. "If the rats have left, the
museum won't need cats anymore. I think
it's quite serious, actually."

"No more rats, a-ha-ha-ha-ha-ha! Oh,
curl my whiskers.
You two'll be the
death of me."
Grandpa Ivan
wiped the end
of his tail over
his one watery
eye and sighed
shakily. "Dear
ones, there are
rats all over this
museum. Everywhere! You may not
have seen them, but that's only because

they're sneaky—and you aren't."

"Yes, we are," Tasha said, annoyed. "I'm very sneaky. I have striped camouflage. And Peter's a black cat—that's the best kind of coat for hiding. We're very sneaky indeed, Grandpa, thank you very much!"

❀ Chapter Eight ❀

Hunting for Rats

"Not sneaky. Honestly," Tasha growled as they stomped away. Or rather, she stomped, and Peter padded after her, not quite sure why she was so upset.

"Maybe you'll be sneakier when you're bigger," he said, trying to be comforting as they popped up out of the hole behind the mummy case in the Egyptian Gallery. He snuffled a sneeze at the strange, musty smell.

"I'm sneaky now!" Tasha mewed, glaring at him furiously. Then her whiskers drooped as she realized just how much noise she was making. "Maybe I'm not." She sighed. "Maybe Boris is right. Maybe I do spend too much time making up stories. Maybe I'm not a good hunter at all."

Peter looked at her, a bedraggled little cat with her ears hanging sideways and her tail sadly fluffed, and he felt himself stand up straighter. "Yes, you are! We both are! We're going to find a rat, Tasha.

We are both brave and fierce. And who wants to be sneaky like a rat anyway? Come on!"

"Okay." Tasha nodded excitedly, her ears perking up again. "It's almost closing time. The rats come out when the visitors leave." She gave a little shudder, and the hairs lifted up all along her spine. "Ma will notice when we're not back for dinner, but I don't care. Which way are we going?"

Peter glanced around desperately. He hadn't actually figured that out. Then he closed his eyes and tried to concentrate. Herring had said that his nose was exceptional. And the other cats were certain that there were rats all over the museum. Surely, he should be able to smell them!

Tasha huddled closer to him as he sniffed the air. Somehow the gallery seemed to be getting darker and stranger with every passing moment. She did want to hunt out a rat. She did. It was just … she hoped it was going to be a small one.

Over on the other side of the gallery, a set of trembling whiskers emerged from a crack in the floorboards, followed by beady black eyes and twitching ears. Another rat appeared behind the first, and then another and another.

"Little cats," the first rat whispered.

"Very little."

"But tasty…."

"Fur gets in your teeth," the last rat growled.

Peter's eyes opened wide. "I'm sure I can smell a rat!" he whispered to Tasha, taking a few steps out into the gallery. "Or maybe even a bunch of rats," he added, sounding a little worried now.

"Ohhh-ooooh…," Tasha squeaked. "I mean, oh, good!"

Just then, the main lights turned off—it was closing time. The two kittens blinked, but their night vision was good enough to see properly even in the dim emergency lighting. The darkness did make everything feel more serious, though. They were real hunters now. The greenish lights shone here and there on the gold-painted mummy cases, but most of the gallery was in deep in shadow.

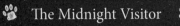

"Come on," Peter said. He was hoping that Tasha couldn't see how trembly he was feeling. But she really wanted to catch a rat, and he was going to find one for her. He was sure he could smell them—in fact, he thought the scent was getting stronger.

Over on the other side of the gallery, the line of rats crept forward, their tails hissing over the boards.

"What was that?" Tasha asked suddenly.

Four rats froze....

"I didn't hear. Oh! Maybe I did…." Peter looked around. There was definitely a noise—but he couldn't tell where it was coming from. Somewhere outside the gallery? But the rats were closer than that, he thought. They smelled really scarily close…. Should they follow the smell, or the noise?

"I'm sure it sounds like little ratty claws," Tasha said, hurrying toward the door.

Peter stood listening, his whiskers swiveling, ears pricked. "Yes…," he breathed. "You're right. I can definitely hear something creeping around."

The kittens hurried out of the gallery, following the rustling noises. Peter nodded respectfully to the bronze cat goddess in the case by the door and tried not to imagine that she was watching him go. Then again, she might be happy with them. She probably didn't like rats, either.

They padded away into the Roman Room, and four rats peered after them, whiskers bristling with disappointment.

"What happened there?" one of them muttered, annoyed.

"Our dinner went galumphing off, that's what happened."

"Four kittens now, did you see?" snickered the largest rat. "Orange, white, tabby, and now a black one, too. So many little cats…."

All the rats nodded and muttered
and hissed as they crept back into their
tunnels.

Peter and Tasha were so determined to
hunt down whatever it was making those
rustling noises that they ran right over
the feet of a statue sitting on the steps of
the Roman temple—and then the statue
woke up and muttered something about
"Rotten kittens everywhere!"

"Was that the Night Guard?" Peter
whispered as he and Tasha raced past.

"Yes. I told you he was grumpy. Usually
he whistles so we know to avoid him.
Don't worry—he was half asleep. He has
to keep walking around all the galleries to
check for burglars, but he stops for a nap
every now and then. I bet that means that

dinner is going to be late. Ma might not even notice we're gone!" She paused, her ears swiveling. "Listen! Can you hear it? That rustling again?"

Peter strained his ears. Yes…. There was definitely something making scratchy little noises up ahead. But the strong ratty smell had died away. He was very confused, but Tasha seemed to know where she was going.

"It's coming from the Dinosaur Gallery, I think." Tasha nodded. "That makes sense. The Night Guard likes to sit in the Dinosaur Gallery to eat his midnight snack. He leaves his sandwiches in a bag under the guard's chair—Boris is always sniffing around them, but Ma says he has to leave them alone. The rats are probably after the sandwiches, too."

They crouched low to the ground and crept into the Fossil Room, every whisker shuddering with excited terror. Then Peter stopped just before the door to the Dinosaur Gallery.

"What do we do if we catch one?" he whispered.

Tasha stared back at him, looking confused. "Um. I don't know. Maybe— call for Grandpa Ivan? Or Ma?"

"Okay. Let's go then," Peter said bravely, and shoulder to shoulder, they tiptoed into the Dinosaur Gallery.

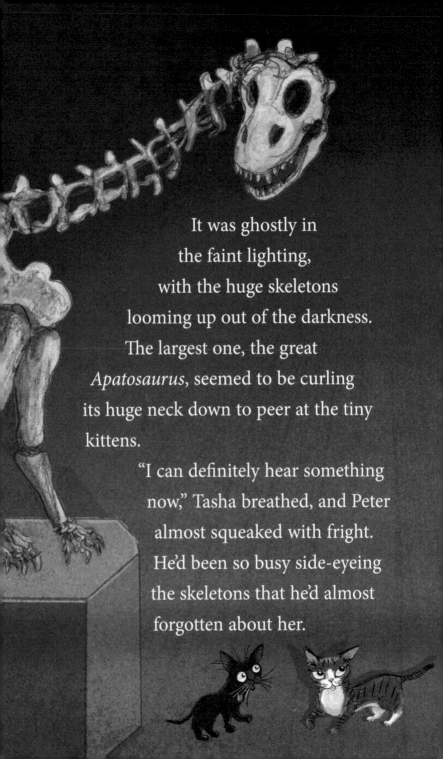

It was ghostly in
the faint lighting,
with the huge skeletons
looming up out of the darkness.
The largest one, the great
Apatosaurus, seemed to be curling
its huge neck down to peer at the tiny
kittens.

"I can definitely hear something
now," Tasha breathed, and Peter
almost squeaked with fright.
He'd been so busy side-eyeing
the skeletons that he'd almost
forgotten about her.

He gulped in a deep breath and tried not to show how scared he was. Yes, Tasha was right. There was a soft, quiet scratching up ahead.

"Over by the *Tyrannosaurus*," Tasha said, her tail flicking wildly from side to side. "Can you hear?"

"Yes. Is it a rat?"

"It has to be. I'm sure it's bigger than a mouse." Tasha crept along beside the *Apatosaurus*'s base and Peter padded after her, ready to spring on the rat.

Tasha was definitely better at listening for strange noises than he was, but he was sure he could catch a rat—he was going to give it his best try, anyway.

"I can hear it now!" he whispered. There was a soft chomping sound and a squeaky rustle. Something was eating the Night Guard's sandwiches!

"Hey!" Tasha mewed. "Leave those sandwiches alone, you thieving rascal! They don't belong to you!"

Peter closed his eyes, let out a wild yowl, and leaped forward, pummeling the rat with his paws. It was surprisingly big. Definitely bigger than he was. Luckily, it seemed to be so surprised by the attack that it wasn't fighting back. Yet.

Tasha was bounding around, trying to

grab the rat's tail and uttering fierce little growls. "See! We're sneaky! We are! We got you, you sneaky rat! Don't you dare eat another mouthful!"

"Hey!" the rat yelled at last. "Get off! Hey, Tasha, get off my tail! What are you doing? I'm not a rat!"

Peter pulled back his paw and peered at the rat in the dim light. It was furry … and striped … and orange….

Their rat was Boris!

🐾 Chapter Nine 🐾

Disaster in the Dinosaur Gallery

"What do you two think you're doing, jumping on me like that?" Boris yelped. His ears were pressed flat against his head, and his tail was three times its usual size.

He was just as scared as they were, Peter realized suddenly.

"This is all your fault, isn't it?" Boris glared at Peter. Now that he figured out that he wasn't being attacked by a bunch of starving rats, he was starting to get angry.

"We weren't the ones stealing!"
Tasha snapped back. "How could you
eat those sandwiches, Boris? That's the
Night Guard's midnight snack! He'll
be furious!" She peered into the little
canvas bag where the guard kept his
sandwiches. Boris had pulled it out from
under the chair, and the foil wrappings
were all undone. The sandwiches smelled
wonderfully of ham.

Boris did look a little ashamed for a
moment, but then he shook his whiskers
and shrugged. "He'll just think it was a rat—
like you did." He smirked at Tasha, showing
his pointed teeth, and she hissed angrily.

"You're so—so—so clueless! The Night
Guard will see his sandwiches have been

nibbled, and he'll think that we museum cats aren't doing our job! That's Ma and Grandpa and the uncles and aunts … and they work so hard." Tasha was so angry that her fur was standing on end, and Boris looked down at his paws. He obviously hadn't thought any farther than wanting a delicious ham sandwich.

"I was trying to show Peter how to catch a rat, and you've just spoiled everything!" Tasha went on, and Boris straightened up.

"Him! I might have known. Why are you bothering? He doesn't belong here. We don't need him."

Peter stepped backward, almost bumping into the *Tyrannosaurus*'s base. He had to put some distance between himself and Boris—the orange kitten was only saying what Peter had said to himself, but his words felt like sharp scratching claws. They really hurt.

"Don't you dare run away!" Tasha snapped, whirling around. "Get back here! I'm trying to prove you're a proper museum cat, and you just give up and disappear!"

Peter stared at her helplessly. If one kitten thought he belonged and one was absolutely certain he didn't, which one should he listen to?

"Look at him!" Boris jeered. "Can't he stand up for himself, Tasha? Does the poor little kitten need you to do all his fighting for him?"

"He knocked you over!" Tasha pointed out.

Boris decided to ignore that. "You're both useless."

"Hey!" Peter felt his whiskers bristle. He still didn't feel like a proper museum cat, but he knew Tasha definitely was one. And she'd been kind enough to try to help him. He wasn't going to let Boris call her names. "You don't get to say things like that—you're just a common thief. It's not enough to take more than your share at meal times, huh? You have to steal food, too?"

"I'm growing!" Boris protested. "I have to eat more than the others."

Peter could hear Tasha squeaking with laughter, and it made him feel taller somehow. "Maybe that's why you don't want another kitten around, because you're worried there won't be enough food! You're just greedy!"

"No, I'm not!" Boris yelled. He launched himself at Peter in a wild, flying jump.

And missed.

Peter and Tasha turned slowly to watch as Boris soared through the air. About halfway through the jump, Boris seemed to realize what he'd done, and he tried to pull back. For a second he swam in midair, all four paws pedaling wildly.

But it was no good. The heavy, solid, large orange kitten crashed right into the *Tyrannosaurus*'s bony tail.

Boris hung there, scratching at the smooth bones with his claws, and then he dropped down onto the base, shaking his orange ears and peering dazedly at the other two kittens.

"Are you all right?" Peter asked, putting his paws on the edge of the base and peering up at him.

"I think so," Boris muttered. And then he added, "Ow!" as a small bone fell on his head. "Ow! Ow! OW!" Another bone fell, and another, and another—until Boris was sitting in a small pile of bones and half the *Tyrannosaurus*'s tail had disappeared.

Boris shook himself and looked at the bones scattered all around him. "Oops!"

"That's not good," Tasha said, putting her paws up next to Peter. "Oh, that's really not good."

Boris looked at her hopefully. "We couldn't just ... sort of hide them behind the curtains?" he suggested. "Would anybody actually notice?"

"Yes!" Tasha glared back at him. "Of course they would. This is the most popular gallery in the museum—and this is the most popular dinosaur. I don't know why. It has useless paws."

"I'll bet the visitors like the teeth," Peter suggested. This dinosaur did have enormous teeth, some of them almost as long as a kitten's tail. Was it his imagination, or was the *Tyrannosaurus*'s head turned a little more toward them than it had been before? The long, sharp teeth and the huge empty eye sockets seemed closer than they had been a moment ago. Peter knew the *Tyrannosaurus* was only a skeleton, but he could have sworn that the enormous dinosaur was not happy.

"So…." Boris poked the bones with his paw, and they rattled together spookily. "You think we should put it back together? That might be a bit … tricky."

"I can't believe you did this," Tasha

muttered, jumping up next to him to look at the bones.

"It's his fault." Boris nodded at Peter. "I was supposed to land on him. He moved."

"I didn't! You just missed by miles," Peter protested. "Anyway, why should I have to stay still and let you squish me?"

Boris shrugged. "I suppose you're right."

Peter jumped onto the base to join them. He peered at the pile of tail pieces and then up at the big gap in the middle of the *Tyrannosaurus*'s tail. "It's all supposed to be held together with those wires," he pointed out. "We just need to thread the bones back on. In the right order."

"But there are so many!" Tasha wailed.

"And the Night Guard will be coming around soon."

"Then we'd better get on with it," Peter said grimly. It wasn't his fault that Boris had crashed into a dinosaur, but it wouldn't have happened if he hadn't been there. He didn't want to give the museum cats a reason to throw him out.

He blinked and thought about what that meant. The museum belonged to him, too. He wanted to stay.

❧ Chapter Ten ❧

A Plan

Tasha hopped down from Boris's back, where she'd been balancing, and peered up at the *Tyrannosaurus*'s tail with a frown. She'd been threading tail bones back together for what felt like hours. Pretty soon the Night Guard was going to show up—or Ma was going to come looking to see why they'd missed dinner. She wasn't sure which would be worse.

"Are you absolutely sure there isn't another bone?" she asked Peter. "There's a hole in that tail. Look."

There was—a big hole, too—right in the middle, where nobody was going to miss it.

"You stuck it together wrong," Boris said accusingly. "Ow, Tasha, you're too heavy. My bones are going to fall apart in a minute."

"We can always leave you to figure it out by yourself," Peter suggested. "Go ahead if you don't want us."

"I didn't say that," Boris muttered sulkily. Then he added, "Thank you for helping me," in a very fast whisper that anyone who wasn't listening carefully would have missed.

"What on earth are you doing?"

All three kittens had been staring up at the gap where the missing bone should be. Now they whirled around in panic, and another bone fell out of the tail and onto Boris's head. He was used to it by now and hardly even flinched.

Bianca stood by the side of the base, every hair perfectly in place, looking up at them in horror.

"Did Ma send you to find us?" Tasha asked, but Bianca wasn't listening.

"You broke an exhibit…!" She looked daggers at Peter.

"It wasn't Peter, it was Boris," Tasha said swiftly. "He banged into it."

"Oh…. Surprise, surprise." Bianca glanced behind her. "But you have to fix it. Now! The Night Guard is in the Egyptian Gallery, and he'll be here any minute."

"We can't," Peter explained. "There's a bone missing. We've looked everywhere for it."

"This is even worse than the Night Guard thinking we let rats eat his sandwiches!" Tasha wailed. "This is a disaster. We never damage the exhibits, never, never, never. It's the most important rule!" She huddled down into a little ball and shuddered.

Boris was still sitting under the *Tyrannosaurus* looking a bit dazed, and Bianca was twitching her tail in panic. Peter laid his ears flat, thinking hard. They had only moments before the Night Guard came by. Somehow, they had to disguise the big hole in the dinosaur's tail. "Maybe we can use something else to fill in the gap for now," he muttered.

"Something else like what?" Bianca demanded, looking around. "There isn't anything!"

"Something white, and about the size

of—the size of—" Peter broke off, staring at Bianca.

"What? Why are you looking at me like that?" The white kitten stepped back nervously.

Peter prowled toward her, eyeing her white fur. Bianca squeaked, twitching her fluffy tail away from him. "Leave me alone!"

Peter shook himself. "I'm sorry—I didn't mean to scare you. It's just—you're the same color as the bones!"

Bianca scowled. "Yes, I'm a white cat. Obviously. I have beautiful fur. Is this really the time?"

But Tasha had looked up and was eyeing Bianca, too. "She is! She's the same color! Oh, Bianca, you can be the bone!"

"I beg your pardon?" Bianca said.

"She needs to hurry," Peter said, his ears stiffening up straight. "I can hear the Night Guard whistling. Quick, Boris, shove his sandwiches back under the chair. We don't want him noticing that they've been moved. He needs to be in and out of this gallery as quickly as possible."

Boris made a wobbly jump down to the floor and pushed the sandwiches back. Then he sat by the chair, shaking his head from side to side.

"Is he all right?" Peter whispered to Tasha.

"He looks fine to me," Tasha said. "Anyway, this is all his fault. He deserves to have a headache. We can figure him out later. Right now, we need to get

Bianca up there, somehow."

The Night Guard's whistling was getting closer and closer, and the two kittens looked hopefully at Bianca. The white kitten glared back, her blue eyes haughty.

"I really don't know what you two are talking about," she hissed. "But I don't like it."

"We need you to be the missing bone," Peter explained. "You can hold on to the skeleton with your claws. It'll be easy, honestly."

"Just for a minute or so while the Night Guard shines his flashlight over the skeletons," Tasha put in. "Otherwise, he's definitely going to see the hole."

"I don't look anything like a dinosaur bone!" Bianca said, horrified. "It's all dirty and old and—and lizardy!"

"It's only for a minute," Peter pleaded.

"No!"

"Of course you don't look anything like a bone," Tasha said, gently bumping noses with her sister. "You're so much prettier. And your fur's all sparkly white, not yellowish like a bone. Oh, Peter, I don't think it's going to work! It's just impossible. The Night Guard will never think Bianca is a bone. Not even Bianca could act that well." She saw Peter open his mouth to argue and dropped one furry eyelid in a slow wink.

"Oh—um, no. You're right." Peter sighed heavily. "We're sunk. I thought Bianca was going to save us all, but it's just too hard, even for her." He glanced sideways at Bianca—were they being too obvious? But the white kitten was preening and fluttering her whiskers.

"I am a very good actress," she purred. "Maybe I could try." She stepped delicately onto the end of the *Tyrannosaurus*'s tail and walked up to the hole, sniffing disgustedly at the bones. "They smell…," she muttered. Then she hopped up onto the skeleton, gripped the wire tightly, and twitched her tail to look as bone-shaped as she could. "There. How do I look?"

"Perfect!" Peter breathed. "You look

exactly like a bone. Except much, much more beautiful," he added hurriedly.

"Just hold on tight, Bianca," Tasha whispered. "The Night Guard is coming. Boris, Peter, hide!"

The three kittens slipped away to the corner of the gallery and tucked themselves in the shadows behind a fire extinguisher. Peter and Tasha huddled

together, shaking with nerves as the
Night Guard stomped in, waving his
flashlight.

"I hope Bianca remembers to close
her eyes," Tasha hissed worriedly as the
flashlight swept over the *Tyrannosaurus*.

The flashlight beam passed over
Bianca, then stopped and came back, and
Peter's whiskers trembled. Had they been
found out?

🐾 Chapter Eleven 🐾

Grandpa to the Rescue!

But the flashlight beam passed on by, and the Night Guard kept on whistling—and then, at last, he walked away.

"We did it!" Tasha mewed. "Is he really gone?"

"Yes," Peter reported back from the doorway. "He's headed to the volcano exhibit. We're safe!"

"Until he comes back," Bianca pointed

out. "Owww, my claws ache from holding on. This skeleton is very, very bony." She dropped down onto the base and shook out her paws delicately.

"You did so well," Tasha told her, purring and sniffing at her sister lovingly.

"But Bianca's right," Peter said. "We've only got—what, another hour until the Night Guard comes around again? We have to find that bone."

"And we should make sure Boris is all right," Tasha remembered. "Boris! Where are you?"

"Here…," Boris mumbled. "I'm fine. Just a little dazed. A lot of dinosaur fell on me, you know. Wait! Someone's coming!"

All four kittens froze. Had the Night

Guard noticed something odd after all? Was he coming back to check?

But instead, a tall white cat came pacing through the doorway and eyed them sternly.

"Grandpa Ivan!" Tasha purred, running to brush her whiskers against his.

"Just what have you kittens been up to?" her grandfather demanded. "Your ma's off on her shift guarding the museum, so she sent me to find out where you all were. You should be asleep." Then his gaze sharpened, and he hurried over to the

Tyrannosaurus skeleton. "There's a hole in this dinosaur!"

"There are a lot of holes in it," Boris pointed out, but then he ducked his head as everyone turned around to scowl at him.

"What happened?" Grandpa Ivan sighed.

"I might have … bumped it. Just a little bit," Boris admitted.

"So what happened to the bone?" Grandpa Ivan looked around as if he hoped to find it lying on the floor somewhere.

"We can't find it." Peter sighed. "We've looked and looked, but the bone just isn't anywhere." He glanced at Tasha. "Maybe a rat stole it."

Grandpa Ivan snorted.

"You did say they were everywhere," Peter protested.

"They only steal things they can eat— or swap for more food. I don't think any sensible rat is going to want a piece of a *Tyrannosaurus* tail. No, it must be here somewhere." Grandpa Ivan strolled all around the base, sniffing thoughtfully. "I can smell ham," he said at last, stopping to sit down in front of the kittens with his puffy white tail wrapped around his paws.

"It's the Night Guard's sandwiches," Tasha said, glaring at Boris. "That's what started all of this."

"They do smell so good." Boris sighed, and Bianca narrowed her eyes.

"You're drooling, Boris. Stop it."

"I can't! I'm hungry. Couldn't I just eat the rest of the sandwich that I started?" Boris looked hopefully at the others. "It already has one corner nibbled off. So really it would be better if I ate it all up. Don't you think?"

"No," chorused Tasha, Peter, and Bianca, but Grandpa Ivan pricked up his ears.

"So, Boris … you opened up the sandwiches?"

Boris hung his head sadly. "I couldn't resist it. I'm sorry, Grandpa."

"And that was before you launched yourself into this dinosaur?"

Boris's whiskers were practically trailing on the floor now. "Yes," he whispered.

"And you've looked everywhere for this bone? All of you?"

The four kittens nodded. They really had.

"It isn't anywhere," Tasha said, shaking her head in frustration.

"It's in the sandwich bag, you silly kittens!" Grandpa Ivan got up and used one paw to flip open the canvas bag.

There, on top of the sandwiches, was the missing bone, gleaming in the moonlight.

"You found it! You found it!" Tasha squeaked, dancing around the sandwich bag, and Grandpa Ivan yawned widely as if it had all been very easy. But his eyes were sparkling, and Peter suspected that he was rather proud of himself.

"So, when we told Boris to put the sandwiches away—the bone was there all the time? Boris, didn't you see it?"

Boris shook his head slowly. "No…. But I wasn't paying much attention at the time. I suppose I could have missed it. Um—I'm sorry, everyone…." Then he caught Tasha's eye and sidled up to Peter. He rubbed his face apologetically against the black kitten's neck. "I shouldn't have said those things, about you being skinny…. And not belonging here…. It was mean."

Bianca nodded. "If you hadn't thought of me pretending to be a bone, the Night Guard would have caught us for sure. Of course, it all depended on my amazing acting skills, but it *was* a good idea."

Grandpa Ivan stared at her thoughtfully, and her whiskers drooped. "And I'm very sorry I was mean," she added, shuffling her paws.

Grandpa Ivan glanced into the moonlight shadows and out through the doorway. "There's a little time before the Night Guard comes back. First we'd better fix this dinosaur." He peered up at the skeleton thoughtfully and then stood creakily on his hind paws to nose the bone back into position. The kittens watched admiringly as he twisted the wires with his teeth and then sprang back down. "There. Poor old thing. No more messing around with bones, you hear me?"

"Yes, Grandpa," the four kittens chorused.

"Good. Now come here, all of you. Sit up here with me." He led them across the Dinosaur Gallery to a nest of fossil dinosaur eggs and settled the kittens in between the huge stones. "I want the whole story. Just what exactly have you been getting yourselves into since young whatshisname arrived?"

🐾 Chapter Twelve 🐾

Grandpa Ivan's Story

Grandpa Ivan shook his whiskers sadly. "You are a bunch of very silly kittens." He sighed. "Of course, whatshisname— Peter—should stay."

"I told you." Tasha nudged the black kitten with her shoulder.

"I think I'd like to stay!" Peter said shyly. "I've decided that I like it here. I'm going to be a museum cat when

I'm older." His ears pricked up eagerly. "I might even ask if I can guard the dinosaurs, now that I know how to put one back together."

"This museum is a haven for all cats," Grandpa Ivan said, eyeing Boris and Bianca sternly. "Have I ever told you how I came to be here?"

All three grandkittens stared at him in surprise. "Weren't you born here, Grandpa?" Tasha asked. "I thought you'd been here forever. Oh, you know what I mean," she added when the other kittens snickered.

"It feels like I have been, when the wind's in the east and there's a draft blowing through the basement making my old bones ache. But no. I came here as a kitten, too." He leaned down to brush his whiskers over Peter's nose, and the little black kitten purred with delight.

"I wasn't much older than you. I came from a town farther up the river, but I was too young to remember much about the place. Only that there was a barn and a tabby cat who was my mother." He sighed. "White cats are often deaf, you know. Oh, don't worry, Bianca. I know quite well that you can hear chicken hitting a dish at two hundred tail-lengths. But I think that's why they did it."

"Did what?" Peter nestled closer to

Grandpa Ivan. His creaky voice sounded so sad, and the black kitten wanted to comfort him.

"They wanted to get rid of me, you see. The people there. They must have thought I would be deaf and no good at earning my keep. So…." He glanced down at the four small kittens and hesitated, as though he wasn't sure he should go on with his tale.

"Tell us, Grandpa," Bianca whispered. She sounded different—small and scared, not the proud kitten she usually was. She crept closer to her grandfather, too, and Ivan lay down, curling himself around the four kittens and licking Bianca's nose.

"They threw me in the river, tied up in a sack."

"No!" Peter squeaked, and the other three kittens mewed in distress.

"I was supposed to drown, but for some reason, I didn't. I floated instead, and a child playing on the bank of the river fished me out. Since she wasn't far from the museum, she brought me here. And I became a museum cat. So you see—" he leaned down to touch noses with Peter again—"anyone can belong to the museum, like I said." He purred a little giggle. "Especially if they're good with bones. Now, I promised your mother I'd find you and bring you back home, since it's so far past your bedtime that it's almost time to get up. The Night Guard will be back here on his rounds in a minute or two. Off you go. Promise me you'll go right to sleep."

"What are you going to do, Grandpa?" Tasha asked as the four kittens padded through the dinosaurs to the doorway.

"Oh, just going for a little walk…," her grandfather purred. "My own rounds, you know. Make sure all's safe. A museum cat never really retires, you see…." He sniffed thoughtfully and his eyes glittered, and a large brown rat darted back behind the *Stegosaurus* skeleton, looking worried.

"I'm going to be like your grandpa," Peter said as he followed Tasha down the tunnel to the basement. His tail was high and proud, and he felt like prancing. "A great museum cat, even if no one knows where I came from."

"Poor Grandpa was tied up in a sack," Bianca muttered, shaking her ears and shuddering. "A horrible wet sack. I should be braver, instead of worrying so much about my fur."

"If you didn't have beautiful white fur, you couldn't have saved us earlier on," Peter told her.

"Well, maybe." But Bianca wrapped her white tail around his thin black one, just for a moment.

"Do you think we'll have adventures like Grandpa Ivan one day?" Tasha sighed. "He's so brave."

Peter nudged noses with her gently. "We just did, Tasha. We fixed a priceless dinosaur skeleton. And we did it all without anybody noticing."

"I suppose we did," Tasha agreed. "And we caught a sandwich thief." She glanced over at Boris, who looked a little ashamed of himself. *Although not nearly ashamed enough,* Tasha thought. "Do you think we'll have *more* adventures?" she asked.

"Of course we will!" Boris told her, brightening up a bit.

"But no more pretending to be bones, please," Bianca said sternly as she sprang up onto their tapestry bed. "It's

undignified, even if I did save the day.
Besides, Ma said to me this morning
that it's time we had more rat-hunting
lessons. We'll be much too busy for fixing
skeletons if we're learning to hunt."

"Good night," Peter yawned, twitching
his paws, ready to jump into the jewelry
box.

"Aren't you sleeping up here?" Boris
asked gruffly, looking down at Peter from
the battered old tapestries.

Bianca nodded. "It's chilly tonight.
You'll be cold in that box."

"And you're too big to fit in it," Boris
added. "Not as big as me, of course. But
not far off."

"Oh…." Peter's eyes brightened. "Well,
if there's room."

He jumped up after the other three and
burrowed in between Bianca and Tasha.
The four kittens wriggled comfortably
for a while, padding at each other, so that
Bianca's fluffy white tail covered Peter's
nose, and Tasha's paws were wrapped
around his neck. Boris was on top of him,
like a furry orange quilt, and every time
Peter breathed, all four kittens went up
and down.

When Grandpa Ivan padded back
down the staircase, they were fast asleep,
dreaming of dinosaur bones and rats
and the adventures yet to come....

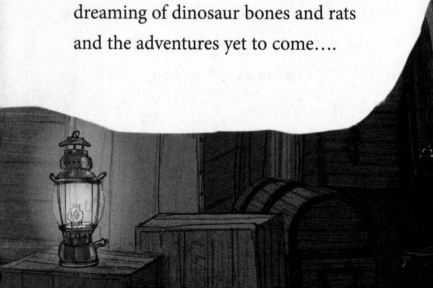

The Real Museum Kittens

This story was inspired by the cats at two museums. There have been cats at the Hermitage Museum in St. Petersburg, Russia, since it was founded in the 1700s. Today, about 50 cats live in the basement of the museum and sunbathe in the courtyards.

For years, the British Museum in London had cats, too. One of the most famous was Mike, who arrived at the museum as a kitten, carried in the mouth of a museum cat named Black Jack.

No one knew where the kitten had come from,
but Black Jack trained him, and he went on to
guard the doors of the museum
for 20 years.

Sadly, the museum no longer has any cats—
except for the beautiful cat statues, jewels, and
mummies in its galleries.

Read on for an extract from Book 2

The Mummy's Curse

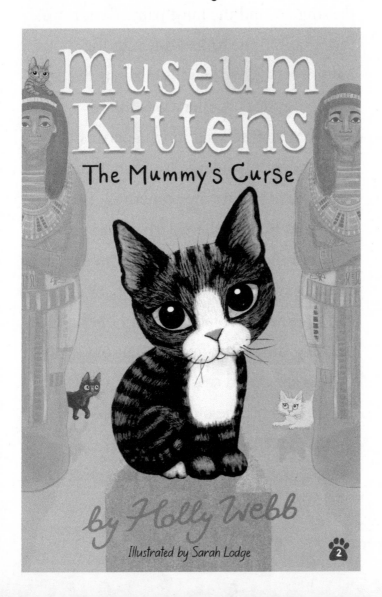

"What are they all so excited about?" Boris whispered to Peter and his sisters. He was peering around the huge painted mummy case that hid the tunnel down to the basement, where the museum cats lived.

The Egyptian Gallery was full of museum staff talking in whispers as they opened up a large wooden crate and started to unwrap something that had been inside. The elderly professor who ran the Egyptology department was actually squeaking with delight.

"Is it jewels?" Bianca asked hopefully, pushing the large orange kitten out of the way so she could see.

"It could be one of those golden masks that the pharaohs had in their tombs," the small tabby Tasha suggested, slinking farther around the mummy case to look. "It must be something very special."

"Gold…," Bianca purred. "Diamonds, too? Maybe pearls?"

"I don't think so," said Tasha. "The masks are mostly gold and lapis lazuli— that beautiful blue stone. The ancient Egyptians used it a lot."

"Hmph! Blue stone." Bianca looked disappointed, and her white tail drooped. "Not as nice as diamonds. But I do like gold."

"*That* doesn't look like a jeweled golden *anything*," Peter pointed out. The black kitten had given up trying to see around Boris and crawled underneath him instead. "It's just … a piece of paper."

"Huh? That's not a treasure!" Bianca said, annoyed.

"What are you looking at?"

All four kittens skittered sideways in surprise as Grandpa Ivan appeared behind them. He was the oldest of the cats, white and long-haired with a great drooping mustache of whiskers. His ears looked chewed, and he only had one eye. But he knew everything that was going on in the museum, and he was very good at sneaking up on the kittens. "Ah, it's here!"

"Do you know what it is?" Boris asked. "It doesn't look very exciting, but the museum people are making a big deal about it. They're putting it in an enormous glass case. Look!"

"It's a temporary loan from a museum on the other side of the country," Grandpa Ivan explained. "They're rebuilding their Egyptian Galleries, so they're lending out their precious exhibits. It's part of the *Book of the Dead*."

"The what?" Tasha squeaked.

"The *Book of the Dead*." Grandpa Ivan chuckled. "It's a set of ancient magic spells for how to safely get to the afterlife, written out on long strips of papyrus. That's paper made of reeds."

Tasha nodded intelligently, and the other kittens tried to look as though they knew what he meant, too. All four of them were gazing at the strange piece of paper in fascination. Ancient magic spells!

"The Egyptians used to put copies

of it into people's tombs so the spirits would know what to do. The scrolls were expensive, though, so they were mostly made for royalty and important officials. This one came from the tomb of a pharaoh, Thutmose I, so it's very grand, with beautiful pictures. This isn't the whole thing, of course. Only a little bit of the scroll is left. All of the tombs were raided by thieves many times—and you can imagine that a long roll of papyrus is quite delicate."

"Hang on…. This is a list of instructions for *ghosts*?" Boris looked shocked.

"Mmm, not quite. I think they'd only be ghosts if they got it wrong," Grandpa Ivan said thoughtfully. "Although no one is quite sure where Thutmose I's body ended up…. He had at least three different coffins. But what's really special about this piece of papyrus is that no one knows what it means. Most of the *Book of the Dead* has been translated— it's all written in hieroglyphics. Picture writing. But this part of the book is tricky to read, apparently, and this is the only copy that's ever been found! I heard the staff talking about it in the café. They're pretty sure it's a spell that has something to do with a magical amulet—or it could be a curse on anyone who steals it…."

HOLLY WEBB

Holly Webb started out as a children's book editor, and wrote her first series for the publisher she worked for. She has been writing ever since, with more than 100 books to her name. Holly lives in England with her husband, three children, and several cats who are always nosing around when she is trying to type on her laptop.

For more information about Holly Webb visit:

www.holly-webb.com
www.tigertalesbooks.com